My Three Best Friends and Me, Zulay

Cari Best
Pictures by Vanessa Brantley-Newton

MARGARET FERGUSON BOOKS
Farrar Straus Giroux
New York

In Class 1-3, there are
22 chairs and 22 desks,
22 pencils and
22 books, 22 hooks
and 22 smocks.
There are 22 people
and 22 names—and
one of them is mine.
Zulay.

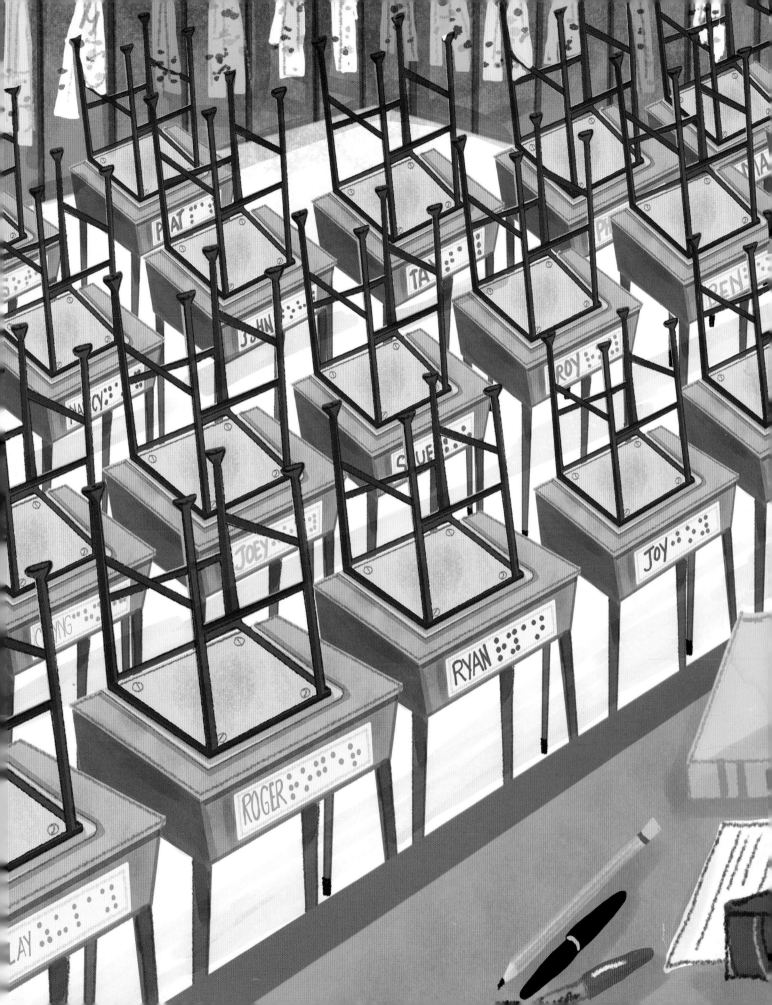

We come to school in our uniform blues by bus, by car, or by our mommas, like me—our blouses ironed, our hair shampooed. Four best friends who help each other, four best friends who help themselves—Maya, Nancy, Zulay, and Chyng.

We link our arms and skip our legs
and sing like the stereo till Ms. Perkins,
the hall lady, tells us to stop.

"You have new perfume!" I say, and she says back,
"Zulay doesn't miss a thing!" which makes me smile
and show my tooth. My tooth that's loose from eating
those carrots that I washed and scraped myself.

"It's time for school," Nancy says, and sure enough, when the shoe shuffling stops, we all line up for two-arm hugs from our teacher, Ms. Seeger, who leads us to our door.

"Good morning, everyone," she says. Then her key clicks the lock for class to begin.

We hang up our bags and take down our chairs and don't care if they land softly or thunder like a stampede.

I feel with my knees for where the chair fits and sit in my seat like Ms. Long at the library—like I can't wait for someone to ask me a question.

Inside my desk there are crumpled papers, pencils, and kisses, and a folded-up cane—a folded-up cane that I push to the back for later.

Then, "My momma bought me new shoes!" I shout. "They're pink she said and good for running."

But I forget there's no talking in Ms. Seeger's class.

"If you have something to share, Zulay, please raise your hand."

So I just think about my new shoes—and try hard not to talk.

Ms. Seeger says: "This morning we'll do shapes and numbers and lots of really good writing. Some of you will get help with math. And some of you will read with me. Then Ms. Turner will work with Zulay while the rest of us go to the gym. And after lunch, there will be a big surprise."

I don't like when I hear my name sticking out there by itself. If no one else has to have Ms. Turner, then why do I? But I don't say the way I feel. I might stick out even more, like a car alarm in the night waking everybody up.

Now it's time for shapes. What's a pyramid? I go and touch it—all five sides—before I draw one at my desk. Up and down and right to left, I hold the pencil with one hand and follow the pencil point with two fingers of my other hand.

"How's this?" I ask, and Maya says, "A teeny bit crooked." So I try to draw it straight. Straight like my cane—my folded-up cane—that's waiting for me in my desk.

Then we do numbers, and Maya says,
"Huh?" So I explain the columns of tens and
ones until she understands.

Writing is next. This is what I type on my Brailler:

One day I'll run, and the wind will push me, and the sun will shine me, and I'll feel like a bird who opens her wings and flies. Only I'll fly with my feet.

Today it's Chyng's turn to type her name on my machine. "The dots feel like goose bumps," she whispers, and I laugh.

"That's how I read," I say. "I see with my fingers."

Reading used to be hard before my hands learned the way. So was climbing a tree—and swimming. Because in the beginning, all I did was fall. And sink. And not want to do it like I don't want to do that cane.

"You'll learn the cane, too," Ms. Turner told me. But she never said it would be a cinch. I know she's here now. My nose knows her Juicy Fruit and the smell of fresh outside.

ZULAY

First Ms. Turner has me feel the cane after I take it out of my desk. That fold-ing hold-ing cold-ing cane.

I open it and fold it and hold it in my lap. I imagine how I look with this thing that no one else has. And I want to shout *"No!"* like I did last time. But instead I try to be patient and get it over and done with.

Out in the hallway Ms. Turner says, "The cane will let you walk down streets, where there are curbs and corners. One day you'll be an expert at finding your way outside— the way you are an expert around your classroom."

Then we practice together in the big outside with no walls or desks or friends. Side to side, side to side.

"Let the cane touch things first. You have to learn to trust it," says Ms. Turner with her Juicy Fruity smell.

My cane finds a tree and my cane finds a car. It snaps back and it gets stuck. Until I say, "I'm sooo tired," which makes Ms. Turner say, "Okay, we can go back inside now."

I am happy to put the cane away, but Nancy wants to try it out.

"No!" I shout. And put it back. At the back of my desk for tomorrow.

After lunch we dance and sing, shaking our heads
and our tails—Maya, Nancy, Zulay, and Chyng—our arms
attached like sausage links as the boys whistle "Woo,
woo, woo!"

Soon we're back at our desks waiting for Ms. Seeger's surprise.

"Are you ready?" whispers Chyng.

"Ready!" I say.

And Nancy says, "*Shhhhhhh!*" way too loud for my ears.

"In three weeks," Ms. Seeger tells us, "we will be having Field Day. There will be contests and races and games outside."

Some people whisper and some people shout. Some even clap, like Maya and me.

"Go home and think about which event you would like to be in," Ms. Seeger says.

And everybody does.

The next morning we sound
like noisy bees. Buzzing and
buzzing and buzzing. Maya would
like to play capture the flag.

Nancy wants to try tug-of-war.

Chyng thinks she can walk holding an
egg on a spoon.
Everyone wants to do something
different.

"And what about you, Zulay?" Ms. Seeger asks.

"I would like to run the race in my new pink shoes," I say—to a class as silent as stones.

Except for Ms. Turner. She's here again. "You go, girl!" she says. "Let's work with your cane on the track."

Then she takes me to the wide outside. The cane jabs
and pokes and snaps.

"Let the cane be your longest finger," she says, "when
you need to know what's coming."

I wonder if I can get it right.

I hear other kids. They're practicing, too. Huffing and puffing and laughing. "This stuff's so hard," someone complains.

And I know just how he feels. Only I'm not laughing because I'm not so sure I can do it.

A few days later I surprise myself. I get from my classroom to the track all by myself walking with the cane.

"Now you're cooking," Ms. Turner says. And I believe that I really am. Then she gives me a stick of her Juicy Fruit gum and I give her a kiss of my chocolate.

"It's time to practice that running!" she says.

We try our best to glue our arms, running ourselves as one. But Ms. Turner and I get all mixed up with our knees and our legs and our feet.

Then one day, after so many days, we finally get it right. Ms. Turner and me, our legs and our feet, all know how fast we can go.

On Field Day everyone is bubbling. I hear mommas and papas and cameras clicking. Friends are here with their "Yays!" My event is the very last, and now it is just about time to start.

Ms. Turner and I stand at the top of the track, so ready to run the race. The smooth round track that I know like my hands. The track that I know like my feet.

"Run, Zulay, run!" my friends all shout, the way I shouted for them. Maya, Nancy, Zulay, and Chyng. Four best friends who help each other, four best friends who help themselves.

So with the wind pushing me
and the sun shining me, I feel
like that bird that went flying.

For Zulay, and for her marvelous mother, too
—C.B.

Vision is something you do with your heart.
For Matthew.
—V.B.N.

Farrar Straus Giroux Books for Young Readers
120 Broadway, New York, NY 10271

Text copyright © 2015 by Cari Best
Pictures copyright © 2015 by Vanessa Brantley-Newton
All rights reserved
Color separations by Embassy Graphics
Printed in China by Toppan Leefung Printing Ltd.,
Dongguan City, Guangdong Province
First edition, 2015
7 9 10 8

mackids.com

Library of Congress Cataloging-in-Publication Data
Best, Cari.
    My three best friends and me, Zulay / Cari Best ; pictures by Vanessa Newton. — First edition.
        pages cm
    Summary: "Zulay is a blind girl who longs to be able to run in the race on field and track day
at her school"—Provided by publisher.
    ISBN 978-0-374-38819-5 (hardback)
    [1. Blind—Fiction. 2. People with disabilities—Fiction. 3. Friendship—Fiction. 4. Schools—Fiction.]
    I. Newton, Vanessa, illustrator. II. Title.

PZ7.B46575My 2015
[E]—dc23
                                                                            2014021833

Farrar Straus Giroux Books for Young Readers may be purchased for
business or promotional use. For information on bulk purchases please contact
Macmillan Corporate and Premium Sales Department at (800) 221-7945 x5442
or by email at specialmarkets@macmillan.com.

Special thanks to Allison Burrows of the Helen Keller National Center
for her assistance with this book.